E
POl

Polushkin, Maria.
Who said meow?

$12.95

DATE		

Who Said Meow?

by Maria Polushkin
illustrated by Ellen Weiss

BRADBURY PRESS / NEW YORK

Bradbury Press
An Affiliate of Macmillan, Inc.
866 Third Avenue, New York, N.Y. 10022
Collier Macmillan Canada, Inc.

Printed and bound in the United States of America

10   9   8   7   6   5   4   3   2   1

LIBRARY OF CONGRESS CATALOGING-IN-PUBLICATION DATA
Polushkin, Maria.
    Who said meow? / by Maria Polushkin ; illustrated by Ellen Weiss.
        p.   cm.
    Adaptation of: Kto skazal "Miau"? / V. Suteev.
    "Substantially revised by the author since its initial publication
in 1975"—CIP t.p verso.
    Summary: Puppy tries to find out which animal makes the new sound
he hears.
    ISBN-0-02-774770-0
    [1. Dogs—Fiction. 2. Sound—Fiction. 3. Animals—Fiction.]
I. Weiss, Ellen, ill. II. Suteev, V. (Vladimir). Kto skazal
"Miau"? III. Title.
PZ7.P7695Wh 1988   87-28073   CIP   AC

To Elizabeth Nina Strachan, with love
—M.P.

For Mollie and Ken, with love
—E.W.

Puppy was sleeping
a sweet puppy sleep.

Meow.

Meow.

Puppy looked under the table.

Meow.
Puppy looked under the bed.

Puppy went outside
and looked
under the porch.
Meow.

Did you say *meow*?

Squeak, squeak. Scurry!
The mouse ran away.

Meow.
No one here.

Meow.
No one there.

Meow.
Must be inside.

Did you say *meow*?

Gr-r-r-r-ow-l-l-l.

Better run, Puppy, run.

Hide, Puppy, hide.

Meow.

Did you say *meow*?

Buzz. Buzz.
Sting!

Yaow-ow-owwwww! Puppy cried.
He ran to the pond and dove in.

Meow.

Was that you? Or you? Or you?
Who said *meow?*

Croak, croak,
laughed the frog.

Splish, splish,
went the fish.

Ssssilly Puppy,
hissed the snake.

Poor Puppy.
His soft puppy fur was wet.
His sweet puppy nose was swollen.
And his puppy spirit was sad.

Home again. Home again.

Meow, meow, meow, again!

Did you say *meow*?

And Kitten said
Meow.